D1243679

JAN ' 2019

# SOPHIE AND LITTLE STAR

Written by Amber Hendricks

Illustrated by Raissa Figueroa

Sophie and Little Star

Summary: When a little star falls from her home in the sky, she finds help from an unexpected friend. Together, the new friends search for a way to send Little Star home, but soon discover that not everyone you meet is kind, or helpful. Little Star begins to wonder if she'll ever find a way home, and if she does, will she be able to leave her new friend, Sophie, behind?

Clear Fork Publishing
P.O. Box 870
102 S. Swenson
Stamford, Texas 79553
(325)773-5550
www.clearforkpublishing.com

Printed and Bound in the United States of America.

ISBN - 978-1-946101-78-5
LCN - 2018948998

To Grandma Loris and Aunt Scottie. And to Hope. This was always your story. - A.H.

For all those who gave me a chance - R.F.

Every night when the sun had set and the

stars gathered in the heavens to shine their light on the

world, Little Star watched, wishing she could join.

But Little Star was far too small and had yet to develop her glow. Besides, it was hard for such a little star to stay up all night!

Each new day when she drifted to sleep,

Little Star would dream of shining her own light.

One morning, Little Star was so sleepy that she stumbled and fell from the sky. Tumbling through the trees, she landed with a terrible crash!

When she looked up, the sky seemed very far

away and she felt very, very small.

Sophie came upon her and asked,

"What is the matter, Little Star?"

"I fell from my home in the sky,
and I don't know how to
return!" Little Star cried.

Sophie smiled and took

Little Star's hand. "Don't worry, Little

Star, together we will find a way!"

Soon the new friends came upon a playful breeze twirling through the trees.

"Ms. Breeze," Sophie asked, "could you please whisk Little Star back into the sky where she belongs?"

Breeze puffed up her cheeks and
blew with all her might.

"Oh no, no, no," she trilled. "I'm much too gentle
to blow that hard. I'm sorry, but I cannot help."

Little Star grew sad. Sophie saw this and said, "Don't worry, Little Star. Together, we will find a way!"

Along the path the pair discovered an oak tree. Sophie
looked at its mighty branches and asked, "Mr. Tree,
will you stretch your branches and lift Little Star back
to her home in the sky?"

Tree lifted his limbs towards the sky, but said with sadness, "Oh no, no, no, my branches are much too short to reach that high. I'm sorry, but I cannot help."

Little Star grew even sadder. Sophie saw this and said,

"Don't worry, Little Star. Together, we will find a way!"

Wandering along, they bumped into a blackbird chasing a worm.

"Mr. Bird?" Sophie asked. "Will you please fly Little Star up into the sky where she belongs?"

Blackbird frowned and
ruffled his feathers.

"Oh no, no, no," he said,
stomping his foot. "My wings are
much too small to fly that far!
Besides, I'm busy!" And he
returned to chasing his worm.

Little Star began to cry. Sophie saw this and said, "Please don't cry, Little Star. Together, I know we'll find a way! **Look!**"

Gathering her courage, Little Star asked one more time, "Mr. Cloud, will you please carry me back into the sky where I belong?"

"Tiny star," replied Cloud. "I am neither mighty like the oak, nor graceful like the breeze, but if you'll let me, I'll carry you home."

Then something amazing happened! Little
Star began to **glow**, and **glow**, and **glow**
with happiness!

But her light dimmed when she
realized she would have to leave her
new friend.

Sophie saw this and said, "Don't worry, Little Star. I will watch where you land in the sky. And tonight, before I go to sleep, I will find you and make a wish!"

Little Star beamed as she climbed onto the
cloud, and together they drifted into the sky.

That night, before she climbed into bed, Sophie looked out her window and found the brightest star in the sky.

Sophie whispered, "Goodnight, Little Star." The star twinkled, and Sophie just knew that Little Star was whispering back,

"Good Night, Sophie."

# About the Author

Born and raised in the Midwest, Amber Hendricks grew up reading everything she could get her hands on-including the morning cereal boxes. That passion melded into writing as well, and by the age of 11 she was writing and binding her own "books". Although she dreamed of becoming a writer, when it came time for college, Amber opted for a more practical major. She earned a Bachelor's degree in Merchandising, with an emphasis on Visual Merchandising, from Northwest Missouri State University. Amber has worn many hats in her career : Army wife, Mother, Visual Merchandiser, Certified Pharmacy Technician, and most recently, Childcare Professional. But she has always circled back to her first love of telling stories. Amber currently resides in Missouri with her husband and two children.

# About the Illustrator

I'm a first-generation Puerto Rican who was born and raised in sunny San Diego. I currently work as a Graphic Designer by day but have been drawing for as long as I could hold a pencil. I'm constantly striving to improve while trying to master the elusive art of adulting. When I'm not making art, I enjoy hiking with my dog Max, trying out new hidden eats around the county, and binge watching new Netflix series.